JUNETEENTH JAMBOREE

BY **Carole Boston Weatherford**

ILLUSTRATED BY

Yvonne Buchanan

LEE & LOW BOOKS Inc.

New York

*To my husband, my children, and
my parents . . . for believing*—C.B.W.

*I dedicate this work to my late uncle,
Raymond Shervington, who, never leaving Harlem,
painted Cowboys and Indians under vast crimson skies,
and other wondrous dreams*—Y.B.

Text copyright © 1995 by Carole Boston Weatherford
Illustrations copyright © 1995 by Yvonne Buchanan

LEE & LOW BOOKS, Inc., 95 Madison Avenue,
New York, NY 10016

Printed in Hong Kong by South China Printing Co. (1988) Ltd.

Book design by Christy Hale
Book production by Our House

The text is set in Goudy.
The illustrations are rendered in pen-and-ink and watercolor
on paper.
The editors gratefully acknowledge the resource provided by "Juneteenth: A Historical Perspective,"
a publication of the Smithsonian Institution's Anacostia Museum.

10 9 8 7 6 5 4 3 2
First Edition

Library of Congress Cataloging-in-Publication Data

Weatherford, Carole Boston
Juneteenth jamboree/by Carole Boston Weatherford; illustrated by Yvonne Buchanan. — 1st ed.
p.   cm.
Summary: Cassandra and her family have moved to her parents' hometown in Texas,
but it doesn't feel like home to Cassandra until she experiences Juneteenth,
a Texas tradition celebrating the end of slavery.
ISBN 1-880000-18-0 (hardcover)
[1. Afro-Americans—Fiction. 2. Texas—Fiction. 3. Family life—Fiction.] I. Buchanan, Yvonne, ill. II. Title.
PZ7.W3535Ju 1995
[E]—dc20   94-26543
CIP AC

AUTHOR'S NOTE

Juneteenth, a blend of the words "June" and "nineteenth," is an emancipation celebration that is said to have begun on June 19, 1865, when Union Army soldiers arrived in Texas and informed slaves that they were free. It took this news two years, six months, and nineteen days after President Abraham Lincoln signed the Emancipation Proclamation to reach the slaves of Texas. Learning of freedom, the joyful ex-slaves set out to find family members from whom they had been separated, and finally follow their dreams.

Over the years, different legends have been created to explain the reason for the delay, including the story that the messenger was sent from the nation's capitol on mule back. Today, African Americans come together all around the country to celebrate Juneteenth with traditions from the early days, including parades, picnics, music, speeches, crafts, and African dance. It is a celebration of freedom and hope.

In 1980, June 19th was made a legal holiday in Texas.

IT WAS A FINE DAY for daydreaming. Breathing in aromas of apple cobbler and tater pie, Cassandra gazed out her bedroom window. Her brother Kufi was in the backyard swinging.

Her mind drifted to the city and the friends she left behind. She liked her new house, and her new school was okay, but what would summer here in Texas hold? This was her parents' hometown, but it didn't feel like home yet to Cassandra.

"Come lend me a hand," her mother called.

Cassandra raced into the kitchen, then stopped in her tracks. Dishes lined the countertop. From the looks of the place, her parents had big plans.

"What's going on?"

"It's a surprise," replied her mother.

Cassandra thought for a moment. It wasn't anyone's birthday.

"What kind of surprise?" she asked.

"A Texas tradition," said her father, as he bent down to kiss the top of her head. "You'll see."

Cassandra helped make red velvet cake while her father fried chicken. Her dad was whistling, and every once in a while he danced over to where her mother was working and twirled her around as if they were dancing at a fancy party. Cassandra loved surprises, and she was usually pretty good at guessing them, but this one had her stumped. She was so deep in thought that she jumped when the doorbell rang.

"See who it is, Cassie," her mother said.

Cassandra could smell her Aunt Bet's rolls even before she opened the door. Texas didn't feel like home yet, but at least it meant that they were closer to family, especially her favorite aunt.

"How's my beautiful niece?" Aunt Bet asked. "Fetch me an apron, would you baby? Then get some cloves from your mama. We've got to get this ham ready!"

Cassandra decided to see if her aunt would give her any clues about what kind of surprise was brewing.

"Are we having company?" she whispered.

Aunt Bet winked at Cassandra's mother and just kept on humming and glazing the ham with honey. "Come on, child. You can help with this part."

Cassandra carefully stuck cloves into the ham and placed pineapple rings on it.

"My, that looks pretty," Aunt Bet sighed as she slid the ham in the oven.

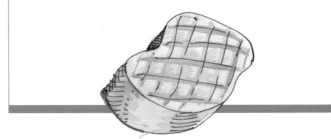

Kufi and Dad busily snapped string beans while Mama began packing a picnic basket. Cassandra had never seen so much food. But she was more curious than hungry. Why the feast? Memorial Day had passed and the Fourth of July was still two weeks away.

"Time to get dressed, Cassie," said Mama.

"But I am dressed," said Cassandra.

Her mother hurried upstairs. "Just you wait," she said, lifting a calico dress from a pine chest. "This is the best part of the surprise."

Cassandra loved to dress up. In fact, her mother sometimes scolded her for going into her closet, and now she was letting her wear this beautiful dress! First her father dancing in the kitchen, and now this! Whatever the surprise was, it was sure making her parents act funny.

She looked in the mirror. The outfit was yellow and blue—the colors of the Texas sun and sky.

"My grandma made this costume for me when I was your age, and surprised me with it on this same day!"

Costume? thought Cassandra. It's not Halloween. Junebugs are jumping and the leaves are all green.

Dad honked the horn. Everyone piled into the car. Cassandra sat next to Kufi on the back seat, holding a cake plate and shooing her little brother's fingers away from the frosting. The car smelled just like the kitchen. All this surprise business was making her hungry!

Within minutes, they arrived downtown. They parked at the church and left the food in the fellowship hall. Then they walked to the square. It seemed like the whole town was there. Some girls from Cassandra's school walked arm in arm in their long skirts and pinafores. Her parents pointed to a banner that flapped in the breeze.

"Juneteenth?" giggled Cassandra. "What kind of word is that?"

"Why, that's the surprise, honey," said Aunt Bet.

"It means June 19th," Dad explained. "That's when Texas slaves heard they'd been freed. President Lincoln signed the Emancipation Proclamation in 1863. But news didn't reach Texas until more than two years later. Nobody really knows for sure what took so long, but you'd better believe folks rejoiced when they finally found out."

"Imagine," sighed Mama.

Cassandra tried to picture what it was like for people to hear such news.

"I bet they sang and danced and had a big barbecue!" she exclaimed.

Fiddlers began to play. Cassandra clapped. Aunt Bet slapped her hip.
"I want to see the ducks!" Kufi begged.
He and Dad walked to the pond.

At a picnic table, Cassandra learned to make a corn-husk doll. "I'll call her Lizzie," she declared.

A girl in a pink pinafore leaned over to look at the doll. "Lizzie's my name too," she said, smiling.

As Cassandra introduced herself, Lizzie's mother called her from another picnic table.

"I've got to go," Lizzie said. "But I'll see you later!" Cassandra hoped so. A Texas summer might not seem so long with a new friend.

"Look, balloons!" yelled Kufi, tugging Dad across the square. The family weaved through the crowd toward the balloon booth. "Can I have one?" Kufi blurted.

"Not so fast," the balloon man said, giving them slips of paper. "First, sign your name."

"But there's already writing on it," said Cassandra. "Forever Free," she read aloud.

"Use the other side," said the man. He slid Cassandra's paper into a balloon, then blew it up while she helped Kufi write his name. "Hold onto it now," he urged, winking.

Under a shade tree, women showed off baskets and brightly colored patchwork quilts they'd made with their own hands. On stage, masked dancers whirled grass skirts to African drum beats.

Lizzie ran over and invited Cassandra to promenade around the square with the other girls in costume after dinner. Cassandra's parents were greeted by old friends they hadn't seen in years.

A bearded man carving a cane spun tales of the first Juneteenth.

"Some folks say the messenger took two years to reach these parts because his mule was slow. Others say slaveowners wanted to harvest one more cotton crop, so they kept the news from their slaves. Me? I don't know whether to blame the mule, the messenger, or the master. One thing is sure, though: Freedom was a long time coming, but it was mighty sweet."

Cassandra heard her father whisper, "Amen."

At noon, the church bells pealed. The high school band marched down the street. A man on stilts towered over the crowd.

A choir sang spirituals that slaves had once sung in the fields. Aunt Bet shook a tambourine and sang along.

As the parade ended, the grand marshal said, "When the cymbals sound, let go of your balloons all at once."

Clash! Clang! Hundreds of balloons, carrying messages of freedom, floated toward the clouds. Cassandra's eyes followed her balloon high up into the sky until she could no longer tell it from the others.

She imagined slave families celebrating their newfound freedom, jumping, shouting, laughing, and crying, their spirits taking wing like birds released from cages.

The balloons soared higher and higher.

In the midst of her daydreaming, Cassandra felt Aunt Bet squeeze her hand, and glimpsed her wiping a tear.

"Don't be sad, Aunt Bet. You'll get another balloon one day."

"I'm not sad, honey—just filled up. I'm so thankful that you're home and we're all together."

"Me too," said Cassandra, giving her aunt a great big hug. "Me too."